PIP AND THE LOST CHILDREN

CHRIS MOULD

Hodder
Children's
Books

A division of Hachette Children's Books

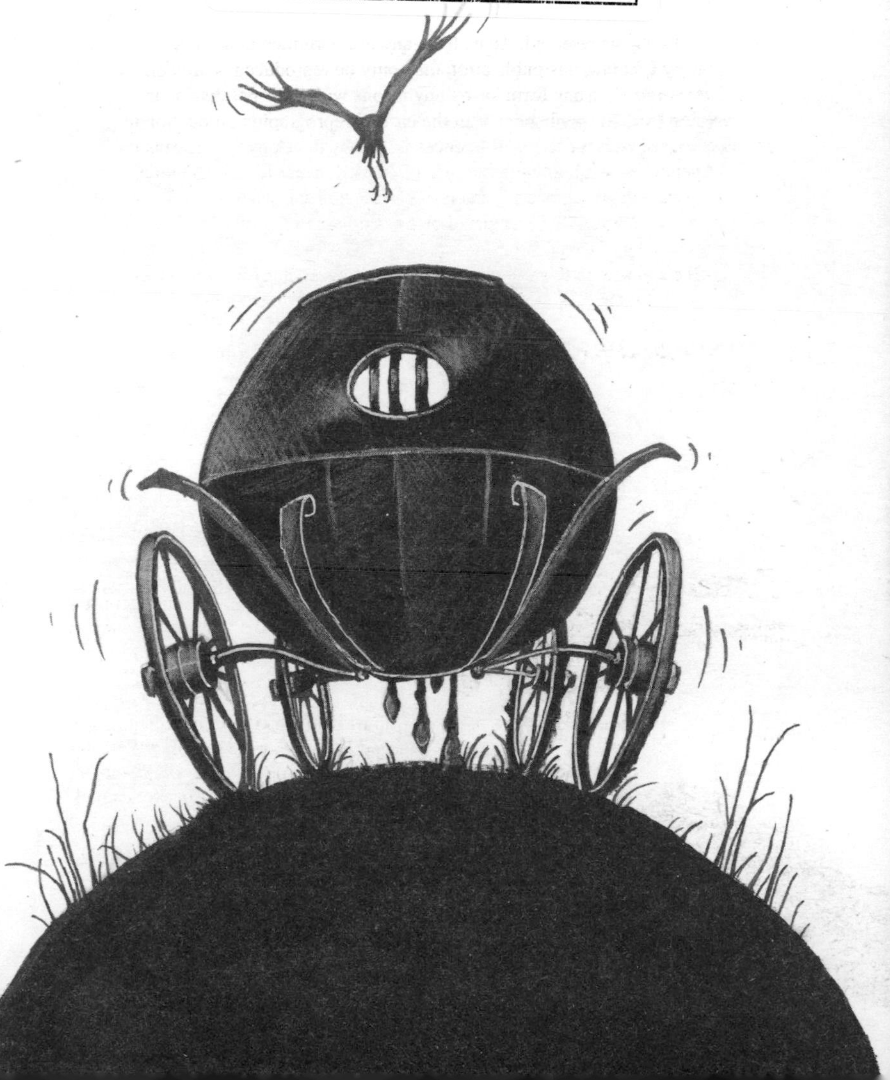

AT WHICH POINT WE RETURN TO THE HOLLOW

Let me take you back through the tall, creaking gates of Hangman's Hollow. Among the blissful winter white snow that lays its cloak gently on the streets and houses, brushing the rooftops and chimneys and wrapping up all its ills, as if to pretend they don't exist.

All those old tales will tell you that there are creatures here. Dark, sinister beasts that emerge from the hollows of the trees and hunt in packs through the cobbled streets and alleyways. Always searching, for the children of Hangman's Hollow. For many years they have come from the woods and darkened the doors of the city to take the little ones. To use them as prisoners in the war against the city.

So it was inevitable that eventually children were forbidden here, rounded up and held in the city keep, away from harm. Rumours abounded of children in hiding and soon the raids began, on homes and buildings all over the city. With men on horseback bearing swords and shields, banging down doors and forcing their way in. And those who had been really unlucky had found themselves in the forest prison.

In the search for lost children Jarvis was appointed city warden. And it was his carriage that you would see rumbling through the streets in the dark hours, searching for the ones he secretly hated the most.

It seemed as if the winter might last forever. The snow and ice held the Hollow captive in its frozen prison and all its doorways were closed to the world.

But if you only looked a little closer, you might see a

different picture. A warm ray of hope, glowing heartily in an attempt to melt the ice. A promise that something was stirring and that things might change for the better.

In the basement of the old Duprie bakery, the bread ovens were roaring away and filling the room with warm air. Slumped on flour sacks and curled up in sleep were fifteen children on the run for their dear lives. They had arrived in an excited state, thrilled at their escape and happy to have found a place of refuge.

Right now they needed rest. Escaping from the clutches of the forest had been tiring work. Pip, Toad and Frankie had rescued the other twelve from the forest prison and they had had to run for their lives until their hearts almost burst from their chests.

No one knew what might come next, but what they did know was that their very existence was enough to put them in great danger.

Frankie had brought them here. The Duprie bakery was her family home, now empty, her parents and siblings held captive by the city. Toad was the boy from the inn, the Deadman's Hand. His father, landlord of the inn, waited patiently for news of his boy. And Pip? Well, in some ways this was all his fault. He had come to the Hollow by accident, escaped from an orphanage many miles away. His arrival had stirred the forest seekers into a frenzy. Children on the move always caused excitement among the woodsfolk.

Pip was fast asleep on a flour sack, blissfully soaking up the heat from the ovens. Toad and Frankie, disturbed from their slumber, sat talking as the others dreamed away beside them. They looked around at the worn-out bodies resting in heaps upon the sacks as their chests rose and fell and they snored in unison.

'Peace and quiet!' whispered Toad. 'I thought they'd never settle.'

Even at the point of exhaustion, the large group of youngsters had proved to be a handful. Their elation at being let out from their forest prison had led to a frantic few hours of chaos in the bakery.

'What now?' said Frankie. 'Where do we go from here?'

Toad stared at her, watching the faint orange light play upon her face in the dark as she spoke. 'I don't know. I'm too tired to think right now,' he said. 'Pip is a good judge. In the morning, when we're all awake, we can make plans.'

'Yes, you're right. Pip will make good sense of it all. We should rest too,' said Frankie.

'Yes, we must,' agreed Toad. 'I'm sorry I woke you – something passed outside.'

Frankie nodded. 'I think I heard it too.'

One boy tossed and turned in his slumber beside them. Edgar McCreedy was the youngest of the children.

It seemed his sleep was fitful too. He had not spent time away from his parents before. Frankie stroked his head and watched him settle again.

'We must all stick together,' she insisted.

'Of course we must,' said Toad, settling himself back into the shape he'd left in the flour sack. 'We are the city's only hope.'

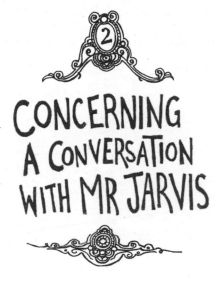

CONCERNING A CONVERSATION WITH MR JARVIS

Jarvis sat with his one hand warming at the fire. He took the hook that made the end of his left arm and skilfully pulled the hair from his face, revealing the scar that trickled down his cheek. There was no going back to being the city warden any more. Not after his troubles with the authorities. He had been caught dealing with the forest folk. The city mayor, Hector Stubbs, had grown suspicious

and so Jarvis had been held in the city prison, until he had managed to escape. His only refuge now was among the creatures and animals of the forest. He lived with them in the wilds of the woods and felt that he had almost become one of them.

'What will you do now, sire?' Esther the crow whispered to him. She was perched on his shoulder, preening her feathers. He took a backward glance at her but he didn't answer.

He was joined by Roach and three of the witches.

They hovered around the fire, rubbing their bony hands, and Roach crouched into an insect-like squat at the flames. A pot of something bubbled and smoked over the flames, held by a contraption made from dead wood.

Jarvis poured the concoction out into a bowl and took a slurp.

'I'll tell you what we'll do,' he began, half in answer to Esther and half addressing the assembled group. 'We will wage war on the city. We will take up arms against them and force our way into their buildings.'

'And then we can capture all their children,' cackled one of the sisters, rubbing her hands even harder and smiling with crooked teeth.

'I want my revenge.' Jarvis scowled. 'If it hadn't have been for those kids from the tavern, I would still have my carriage, my house in the city. I would still have been the local warden and kept my grip on those streets. This is a full-scale assault. We will destroy all of them. But the first thing I'll do is see to those three city rats. Come hell or high water, I'll have my revenge on them. And one day, I shall take up my seat in the mayor's house and rule this place in the way I see fit, and it will never be home to children ever again. Not a single, skinny little wretch. Not one.'

He curled his hook into a nearby trunk and pulled himself up. Esther flapped backwards and lifted herself from his shoulders to take to a convenient branch. 'We will move at night,' Jarvis went on, 'and use the cloak of darkness to our advantage. In the day we rest.' He kicked out the flames of the fire in frustrated anger and wandered away.

As the light from the fire died, darkness poured around them. Roach turned his moonlike eyes to the witches. 'He is right. It is our only hope.' He used his four long arms to help him rise to his feet. 'We must sharpen our weapons and build our carriages of war. The time has come for the forest to meet the city in full force. Let us spread the word to our sisters and brothers.'

A cry filled the air. It could be heard across the city and even the townsfolk knew that it spelled a meeting of the Stone Circle. The witches turned to the air and began to stir up the night sky, flitting across the moon in their ragged cloaks.

A council of war would soon be in session.

THE BIT BEFORE
CHAPTER THREE

In the shallow flicker of light from the bakery ovens, the Captain opened his eyes. *Click click*. His rounded lids rolled back in the semi-darkness. All the recent activity was disturbing his sleep. There was so much to think about all at once. Not long ago he had been wrapped up in hiding in an old cloth sack. But since his discovery his mind had been turning frantically. Everyone wanted to know the whereabouts of the lost children, and only the Captain knew the answer.

One look at Captain Dooley and what met your eyes was a bedraggled wooden puppet, lifeless and limp. But know him better and you would find that this enchanted little fellow spoke of the children in hiding. He knew every hiding place of every single boy and girl.

And that was what made him so valuable. If those forest creatures got hold of him again that would be the end of all of them. But for now, he sat tightly in Pip's grasp, awaiting his next request for information.

Something in particular was rattling his slumber. He kept on dreaming the same dream, over and over. Of the young boy and how he would give them all away and let them down. No matter how much he had tried to ignore it, it wouldn't go away and kept him tossing and turning.

'He will let you all down,' the Captain said out loud in the darkness, half asleep and half awake. 'He doesn't mean to, but he will give you all away and you'll all be in trouble. And then you'll see!' he cried.

But he went unheard in the black of night, his voice drowning in the silence of the sleep of children. And so no one knew what was to come.

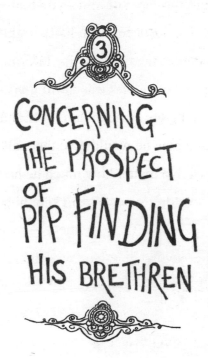

CONCERNING THE PROSPECT OF PIP FINDING HIS BRETHREN

When Pip awoke he looked across the room and the first thing he saw was Frankie fast asleep on one of the old sacks. She was curled up, facing the warmth of the oven, although the fire had almost died. He quietly opened the iron door and slipped more logs inside. The basement was in darkness and so he crept up the short staircase and carefully lifted the hatch to the outside world.

The chink of daylight blinded his opened eyes and he was sure that it must be almost midday. A rumble of street noise filled his ears. He quickly lowered the doorway and wakened Frankie.

'I have something to tell you,' said Pip excitedly, 'about Captain Dooley.'

Frankie opened her eyes slowly. She had slept so deeply in the night that it took her a moment to realize where she was and why. She had to gather her thoughts again quickly, remembering that they had run from the forest with the little ones to escape the creatures of the night and returned to her family home, knowing it was empty and safe. She could see the wooden soldier laid on the sack at the other side of the basement, his seemingly lifeless appearance belying his prophetic abilities. How could anyone know how important he was to the safety of the children of the Hollow? Or realize what information he might hold?

'What is it?' she said, still only half awake.

'Frankie, I have a brother. A twin. There is another Pipkin boy.'

'What?' came Toad's voice from the corner. He had woken with Pip and was only just stirring when Pip's revelation came.

'Listen,' Pip began. 'Late last night I grabbed hold of the Captain for the first time. He knew my name was Eddie Pipkin when I held him, and he told me something. That I am one half of the Pipkin duo.

There are two of me. I have a long-lost brother, a twin.'

'It might be a trick,' announced Frankie. 'A trick to lead us back to the forest, into the arms of the woodsfolk.'

'She's right,' said Toad. 'We don't know what the Captain is capable of. He might be plotting against us.'

'No,' said Pip, growing upset at their idea. 'It's true. I know it's true.

'I know there is something missing. I've always known. I must find him.'

Toad looked at Frankie. They shared a doubtful acknowledgement of their thoughts.

Pip was angry. How could they crush his hopes like that? He was an orphan. He'd never known anything of his family and he had no information about his roots. The Captain had given him hope. He turned towards the doorway that led to the bakery shop.

'No,' said Frankie. 'Stay down here, Pip. You will put us all in danger.'

But Pip took no notice. He only came back to grab the ragged wooden soldier and then, taking him by his arm, he walked up the stairs and headed into the bakery above, slamming the door.

He sat in the shop window for a while. It was boarded up and chinks of light spilled in and cut across his saddened face. Shortly he was joined by Toad and Frankie.

'We have to be careful, Pip,' said Frankie. 'If we give ourselves away or make a wrong move we'll be back in that forest prison, or the city prison for that matter, before you know it. We escaped within an inch of our lives. We're safe for now. Let's just take a while to let the dust settle. We don't know too much about the Captain.'

'But he only tells the truth,' insisted Pip. 'He is neither friend nor foe to anyone. He simply gives what he knows to whoever is there.'

'Don't make it fit,' said Toad.

'What do you mean, don't make it fit?' asked Pip.

'I mean, don't tell yourself what you want to hear. If this is a trick and he leads us all into the hands of Jarvis, you will have that responsibility on your shoulders. Do you understand?'

Frankie walked across and sat by his side. She put a hand on his shoulder and she felt his pain. The thought of finding a brother would be everything to him, she knew that. And what could be more cruel than to tell Pip he had a brother when he didn't?

'If you do have a brother and if he is here, he will be safe, I'm sure. Let's just take our time, Pip. If we rescue him, we need to do it carefully and with a proper plan and the right amount of time. And he might not even be here. He may be somewhere else, in which case he is safe, and as long as we keep hold of the Captain, we'll find him.'

Pip knew they were right. They stood and stared at him, waiting for an answer.

'Just leave me here. I'll be down in a minute.'

'I'll make fresh bread,' said Frankie. 'We need to eat.'

18

She knew this would force a smile from his face and he grinned sideways at her as she turned to go. She and Toad went out of the room, leaving Pip sitting with the Captain in his hands.

THE BIT BEFORE
CHAPTER FOUR

Pip could hear the rattle and hum of the streets outside. It unnerved him to be sitting so close to the noise, as if he could be seen through the boarded-up window. He was about to head back down into the basement, but before he moved he had to ask the Captain something.

'Where is my brother, Captain Dooley? Where is the other half of the Pipkin duo?'

The Captain's eyes opened so quickly his lids made a clatter and Pip jumped momentarily.

'Poor Billy Pipkin. I can see him now, but the picture is unclear. All alone in the Hollow.'

'Where?' cried Pip and he grew angry, holding the little soldier tightly in a vicelike grip. 'Where?'

'The snow blows and the wind howls and I cannot see,' said the Captain and his eyes closed again.

Pip threw him across the room and the wooden toy skated across the wooden floor, landing in a heap

in the corner, his limbs tangled in a lifeless knot.
And then, as if suddenly recognizing his foolishness,
Pip picked him up and made sure he was still intact. He
gripped him in his hands and returned to the basement.

'How long before bread is ready?' he asked Frankie.

'Soon,' she said. 'Real soon.'

REGARDING THE RESTLESS NATIVES OF THE HOLLOW

The sound of woodland noises grew louder. The forest was stirring. Anger was boiling. As night fell, creatures, both two-legged and four, began to work their way into the streets. As far as the woodsfolk were concerned, this was the beginning of the end of Hangman's Hollow. It would not be over quickly. It takes some time to overpower a city so huge. The forest army was well aware of the long task ahead.

'I have sent bark demons into the Hollow,' announced Jarvis to the witches. 'To provoke the city folk into action. To let them see that we mean business and to pull them out of their cosy little holes. Away from their firesides and into the streets where we will do battle.' He grinned and as he spoke he sharpened his hook on a nearby stone. Then, as if to test it, he ran its tip down a strip of tree bark and watched it tear open the tough woody skin of the Spindlewood tree.

'Excellent work, Jarvis. We shall make a presence in the air and stir up the crowds,' said Hogwick, and immediately she soared upwards and attracted followers in tattered shrouds.

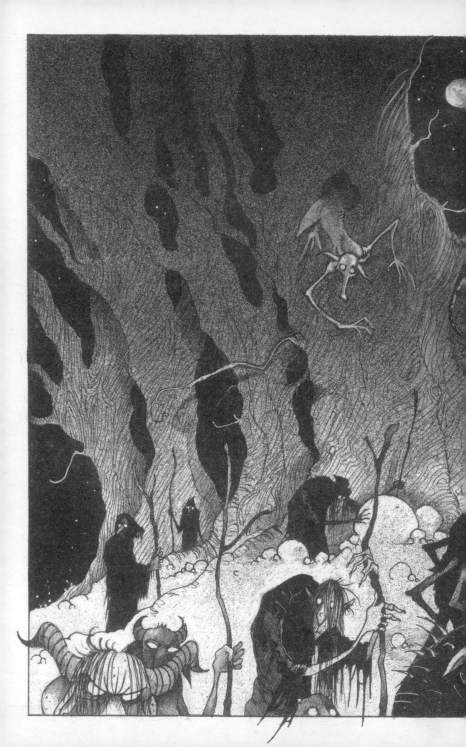

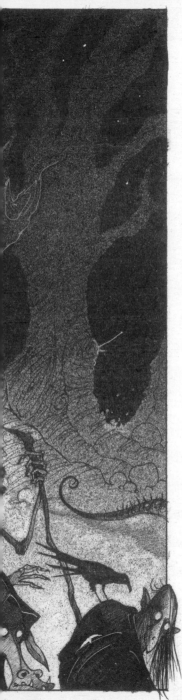

*

Back on the streets the creatures clawed their way down an alleyway, leaving strange footprints behind. They searched with eyes and nose and ears, taking in the smells and sounds of the city and seeking out the chance of nearby flesh. It is quite a sight to come across a bark demon. They have many different forms. These were four-legged and long-snouted. Hard, bristly hairs stood out from the thick hide on their backs and they lurched slowly, using all fours to convert from walk to climb. Their eyes were typical of forest creatures – small and circular with a moonlike glow in the dark.

These were no longer the days of taking prisoners, these

were the first days of war, when those of the woods had permission to be rid of their enemy. To be found on the streets in the following days would be a fatal mistake for the city folk.

The snow had come again and it covered the giveaway signs of those, good or bad, two-legged or four, who dared to venture out.

One demon clawed its way around the icy cornerstones of a nearby building and slipped between the rotten core of wood that made the doorway, pulling its structure apart with clawed digits.

It sniffed the air. There was something in here, for sure. A noise came from behind, and the demon was joined by the others. The scent of flesh filled their noses and the beating of hearts resounded in sensitive ears. Silver glowing pupils peered through blackness and found their way into the corners. They drew closer and sounds could be heard. Small feet, moving swiftly.

Rats. Hordes of them, picking away at something rotted and dying. The seekers forced their way back outside through a boarded-up window and returned to the falling snow.

They had only to chance upon an occupied building and they would not hold back. For so long they had had to resign themselves to making prisoners of the children, when they found them. The sight of them holed up in the forest keep had frustrated their animal instincts for what seemed like forever, while they fed on meagre scraps. But now was their hour.

'Let all hell break loose!' said Jarvis to an assembled group in the forest. And he laughed a sinister laugh that rang out into the night. 'Do what you will. Feed upon the flesh of the city. Take what good you can from their bones and blood and let us have reign over Hangman's Hollow.'

Jarvis watched the creatures rouse themselves into a frenzy. He rubbed his hands together and turned to look upon his shoulder, where Esther sat obediently.

'Esther, you know what I want. I want those children. You are my eyes and ears. Go now and see what you can find.'

'WHEN THE WORDS 'STUBBORN DETERMINATION' ARE USED

In the heart of the bakery the ovens were keeping the basement warm. The young ones were running around the room, burning off their energy and tiring themselves out.

'Quiet!' urged Frankie. 'That wood will not last forever. It doesn't need to be roasting hot in here all the time. We need to learn to be more careful. We don't want to be venturing out and searching for firewood when it's not necessary. There's hardly any left.'

Pip watched Frankie and listened to her. He had watched her grow from being a frightened, speechless captive into a brave young escapee, capable of taking control of the group and showing good sense and management.

'What are you staring at?' she asked.

'Oh, I'm just listening to you rabbiting on,' he jested. 'Is it all right if I warm my hands at the oven door? I don't want to take up all the heat.'

'Shut up,' she returned, smiling. And she threw something at him that missed.

Just then a noise came above them. Something walked over the trap door to the basement. They all froze in fright, silence finding its way quickly around the room. Young Edgar was about to stir, the look of a frightened cry ready to burst from his mouth. Frankie looked across the room at him. She did not dare to move. Holding her finger to her lips she mouthed something to him that seemed to keep him calm. She had a way of easing his young mind, mothering him in her caring way – something the others were unable to do.

There was a scratching of some kind. Perhaps someone was trying to lever the hatch or scrape something over the wooden entrance. Toad held his arms out and signalled to the little ones to keep calm. He wore a reassuring look upon his face as if to show them it would be all right. But inside his heart thumped hard inside his chest. He slowly reached out his arm and lifted a broom in his left hand. It would be inadequate, but it was all he had.

It seemed as if Edgar couldn't hold on any longer. His eyes were held tight shut and a single tear ran down one cheek. There was nothing they could do except stay calm.

With great relief, though, the moment passed. Whatever it was could be heard padding away into the distance.

'City guards,' said Toad.

He could not resist a peek. He pushed the trap door upwards to receive a blast of cold air in his face and find snow covering the ground and concealing their entrance point. He peered across in front of him. There were footprints. Many of them. But they were not the footprints of people. More likely they were the prints of something much more sinister. They had been lucky.

'We need to secure this trap door,' he said. 'So that it can't be easily pulled upwards.'

But Pip's mind was elsewhere. He was thinking of his brother again. Unbeknown to the others he had taken Captain Dooley to one side more than once that day.

Each time was the same. Something stopped the Captain from seeing his brother clearly. And all he kept saying was, 'The whirling wind and snow won't let me see the Pipkin boy. I know he is there, somewhere in the Hollow, yet I cannot grasp him. The information comes and goes. I can see a tower and steps, yet nothing more. Come to the Captain, Billy Pipkin. Come to the Captain.' And then he would drift back into his sleep, closing his eyes gently.

'Perhaps it's the old clock tower,' Pip had said to himself. It was there that he and Toad had rescued Frankie. And he felt sure that even if he went alone, he would be able to find it. With that idea planted in his head, his mind had drifted all day and he was almost unable to think of anything else.

When the children settled down again at the end of the day and had eaten as much bread as their bellies would allow, they lay down upon the sacks again. Perhaps a few more days of lying low and they might move. It made sense not to stay in one place, they thought. They knew that all the empty buildings would be regularly checked. But it would not be easy to move the whole group again. It would be a tense procedure. The little ones didn't run so quickly and they asked too many questions.

'We're down to the last few logs already,' exclaimed Toad. 'We'll need to replenish supplies from somewhere at some point.'

As the night settled in there were noises from above. Horses' hooves rushed over the snow-covered cobbles. Shouts echoed through the streets and all manner of noises came from the direction of the forest. It always seemed that at any moment something might come through the hatch and take them away. If this happened, they would be helpless.

'Tomorrow we should plan our escape,' said Toad.

His suggestion was met with sombre nods of approval from the room. For now they needed rest.

But someone was hell bent on leaving that night. Someone who had the idea of finding his brother. When he thought everyone was asleep, Pip slipped into his boots and edged his way through the basement to the short staircase that lay under the trap door.

Toad had tried to stay awake, half expecting that Pip might make a move. But soon he was in the thick of sleep and snoring rhythmically. Frankie was not so careless. She had rested with one eye still fixed on Pip and now she got to her feet, following him to the staircase.

'Stop!' she cried, pulling on his arm. 'Pip, you mustn't leave. Really you mustn't.'

'I won't put you in danger,' he said. 'I'll be gone from here and I'll return safely. But there'll be two of us, that's all. I'm sorry, Frankie, really I am. But I'll be back. I have to find him. This place is safe. As long as you all sit tight, it will be fine.'

'You will put us all at risk,' she insisted.

'I won't. I'm too careful,' he said.

Frankie was impressed by Pip's brave and stubborn determination, but she didn't let it show.

'Go, then,' she said and she wished him luck, kissing him on the cheek and shoving bread into his pockets as she patted him on the back.

He turned and eased up the hatch, peering through and looking around before lifting it high enough to make his exit. He brushed his footprints away behind him and headed off with the Captain secured at his waist belt.

'Toad, quick!' urged Frankie in her bid to waken him. 'It's Pip. He's gone.'

Toad sat up and rubbed his eyes, looking around the room and gathering his thoughts.

'I knew it,' he said. 'That's why he didn't want to secure the door. He can't do this alone. It's a trap. I know it is.'

'Look, if you join him, we'll be OK here. Just … be careful out there and don't be too long. We'll sit tight until you return,' said Frankie.

'Are you sure, Frankie? It's just that, you know, I don't think he's safe out there alone.'

'I know. It's fine. We're OK. Really we are. Just go.'
Frankie packed up a loaf of bread in a small satchel and
patted Toad on the back as he ascended the stairs.

He turned around at the top.

'I'll see you soon,' he said and he managed a half-
smile.

Frankie smiled and hurried him on, gesturing with
her hand. 'Hurry up,' she said, 'you'll lose him.' And
she turned away, trying not to cry as she watched him
disappear. She was not sure where her tears came from.
Half through fear of being alone and half through the
fear of losing the two boys who had become like
brothers to her in a short space of time.

Toad grimaced at the transformation from warm
cosy fireside to dark and bitterly cold streets. He felt
the chilled air bite at his warm skin as he emerged into
the wintry gloom. A stiff breeze rushed at him, causing
his eyes to water. Lumps of hardened snow pummelled
his feet through his boots and he shoved his gloveless
hands into the folds of his tunic. He had forgotten
exactly how unbearable it was, out in the Hollow. At
first he thought that Pip had disappeared altogether,

but as he perched in a nearby underpass he could see Pip's foggy breath fill the air and the silhouette of his face become clear.

'I thought you'd come,' said Pip. 'I'm heading for the clock tower.'

'Then you're already heading the wrong way,' said Toad. 'Good job I came, eh?'

'But you can see it from here. It's across the bridge.'

'Across the bridge? You'll get us all killed, Pip. Follow me.' Toad set off, confidently winding his way down some side alley that Pip didn't even know existed.

Within moments the boys were making their way towards the other side of the Hollow, with only the moonlight to show their way.

AT WHICH POINT FRANKIE IS ALONE AND IN CHARGE

Two figures were perched on low branches at the edge of the forest. One was draped in a hooded cloak, another was identifiable by his two pairs of arms. They were watching the city with close interest, keeping a silent watch over its movements and making note of its rituals.

The four-armed one pulled himself upwards, moving insect-like between the branches, his moon eyes scanning everything around him. Until now the two had spoken not a word to each other.

'What could be easier?' piped up the cloaked and crouched figure. 'I'll have my hands on those horrible little rats before the spring is here.'

'You mean your hand … not your hands!' came the correction from the branches above.

'What?'

'You said "hands". You only have one hand. The other is a hook.'

'Yes, Roach, thank you. When I need your advice I'll ask for it.'

'My apologies, sire.'

Frankie felt a stronger sense of responsibility heaping itself upon her. She looked around at the sleepers. If anything or anyone came she would have to rouse them all into action by herself. It would be no mean task. She spent the next few hours awake, nursing her anxiety, perched at the edge of the ovens and listening out for sounds of city and forest spilling into the street.

Eventually she realized she was being watched.

Young Edgar McCreedy was awake. He was sitting up straight and staring at her with reddened eyes.

'Where are they?' he asked.

'They're not here. They've … nipped out for a short while,' admitted Frankie, trying her best not to seem too concerned.

'Why have you been crying?' he questioned.

'I haven't. I mean … I … I just miss my family,' she said, forgetting that she would remind him of his own troubles.

'I miss my family too,' he said. 'Why can't we go home?'

'We can't, Edgar. Not just yet,' she said. 'Not just yet. Come and sit here.' Frankie patted down the flour sack and made a space. At first he held back, not wanting to move, but there was something about Frankie that made him feel safe. He trotted across the stone floor and curled up alongside her. They lay in silence and she stroked his tiny face. Edgar listened to her heartbeat and he began to drift into sleep. Frankie was full of worry for the boys – what if the Captain really was playing tricks on Pip? It would be the end of them all if the little wooden soldier lured the boys towards Jarvis or the woodsfolk. It was some time before sleep overtook her.

Edgar stirred from a bad dream. Still lost in sleep, he gazed around the room, disorientated by his strange surroundings. He sat himself up and after a moment he took to his feet, wandering around the room in the darkness, until unknowingly he began sleepwalking up the short staircase that lead to the trap.

Edgar climbed the step and for a moment he was confused as to how to get out. The doorway split in two and needed to be pushed upwards and back to make the opening. Eventually he managed it and wandered out into the night. The streets were familiar, though he had no real idea of where he was.

For a while he wandered aimlessly, growing upset by his own confusion as the cold biting wind worked hard to waken him properly.

He looked down and realized he was out in the snow and ice, his feet now covered in freezing white flakes and his body shaking uncontrollably. Understanding in a moment of panic that he had left the hiding place in his sleep, he quickly found his way back to the Duprie bakery. His own shock at what he had done roused him to his senses.

He traced his steps back to the basement door that lay flat on the ground at the back of the alleyway and lifted the wooden opening before returning inside. Frankie was fast asleep, unaware that her midnight companion had been out walking. Edgar snuggled back into place at her side and filled the dent he had left in the flour sack. The warmth of the bakery basement was enough to settle him, and he eased back into slumber to the sound of the icy wind outside.

A QUIET WORD
BEFORE CHAPTER SEVEN

The two bark demons were perched side by side. They had seen something, and they watched patiently. Their eyes grew wider at the vision before them and their hearts quickened. Their nostrils opened up – the smell was familiar. They had found what they had been seeking.

A small boy out in the street, wandering through the snow, and though it appeared he was only very young, he was all alone.

They watched him. Perhaps he would lead them to the others. So they perched a while and let him lead the way. At first he appeared not to know where he was going. He was headed in one direction, but seemed to become confused and turn back, so, from a distance, they followed him.

He worked his way down a darkened alley, around the back of the old Duprie bakery, and lifted the basement hatch. He looked around as he sneaked inside, perhaps mistakenly thinking that he hadn't been seen.

Above them, Esther squawked as she hovered overhead, before landing nearby. 'I am presuming our eyes have seen the same vision?' she asked.

'Child,' muttered one of the bark demons, and it was only because Esther was used to him that she could understand his strange rasping voice.

'There may be many,' she suggested. 'We should gather in numbers. They'll scatter like rats and we'll lose them again. Let us return to the forest, collect our brethren and return fully armed.'

At that moment, a guardsman turned the corner on horseback. The foresters shuffled into shadow and hid their large frames in the darkness. Esther lifted upwards and perched nearby.

From where she sat she could see everything. The bark demons were quick to pounce, and when they did the guardsman was taken by surprise and became completely helpless. His horse was not quick enough to get away, allowing the demons to take hold with their claws. The snow-filled alleyway ran red with the first blood of the city's victims.

There would be more of this in the days to come. Much more. Esther took to the air and followed the demons' bloody footprints back towards the undergrowth. Jarvis stood in wait.

As the creatures drew nearer he approached them and saw their reddened mouths.

'My, my ... you have been busy already.' Jarvis grinned.

'There is much to tell you,' announced Esther. 'We should gather together and make our advances, and quicker than you might think.'

WHICH SEES THE WOODSFOLK TAKING TO THE DUPRIE BAKERY

Pip and Toad pushed on through the city. Their progress was slow, as they stopped frequently to avoid men on horseback patrolling the streets. The wind howled through them and snow fluttered around their faces. The clock tower would soon be in sight – there was not far to go. Pip checked that the Captain was held fast at his belt.

He tried to whisper to him but his voice went unheard in the howling gale. Perhaps this whole thing was a bad idea.

'Not much further,' cried Toad. His hair blew wildly and he held on to his tunic.

Pip forced his head downwards so that he might make it easier for himself as he walked further. The wind was pushing them back, trying its best to impede them.

The archway under the clock tower was visible now. They checked left and right before crossing the wide cobbled street and venturing inside to where the stone staircase spiralled upwards to the clock-tower door.

The door was secured, but Pip was able to pick at the lock until it sprang open. It was dark and cold and frozen. The gale was blowing snow through a hole in the clock face and a small drift was building up against the wall in one corner.

At first glance the room seemed empty. Pip's face dropped and his heart sank. He had expected to find his brother sitting right there, huddled in a corner, like when they'd found Frankie.

'Don't lose heart,' said Toad. 'We haven't started yet.

We need to search carefully.'
He called out, but no
answer came. He
began to search in
the corners and
Pip climbed
upwards into
the clock
workings to see
if he could see
anything.

Pip continued the calls from his lofty position. But
no answer came. He tugged at his side and removed
Captain Dooley from his waist.

'Captain, where is Billy Pipkin?'

'Not here,' came his answer. 'The Captain can't see
Billy Pipkin.'

Pip shook his head. It didn't make sense. This hadn't
happened before. Captain Dooley should be able to see
the children wherever they were. How long would it be
before the picture became clear and Billy Pipkin was
brought to safety?

But elsewhere, hearts were lifting to good news. A small group had gathered at the side of Jarvis in the forest. Esther took a position on a prominent branch where she might make an announcement. The two bark demons were at her side and Roach was perched insect-like at a small fire.

'What is it, my dears?' asked Jarvis. 'You have important news?'

'We have made a breakthrough,' announced Esther.

'Well, don't beat about the bush, Esther. Don't have us all waiting.'

'It's the old Duprie bakery. They're using it to hide out.'

'They?'

'Children!' said Esther.

Jarvis jumped to his feet and his eyes opened wider. Roach stepped back in surprise. Some of the woodsfolk were already on their heels, as if to head straight to the city without instruction.

'COME!' squealed Jarvis, pushing to the front, clenching his fists and gritting his teeth. 'Join me.' He pulled at his cloak and grinned a wide grin. 'There may be hundreds in there for all we know. And I want to weed out those rats from the tavern. We need a structured attack, a careful approach. But we must move and quickly. Let us plan on the hoof.' He quickened his feet, sharpening his hook on a nearby stone as the others began to follow. Roach grinned and rubbed his hands. The excitement was almost too much to bear.

Toad looked out through a side window. Something moving in the street caught his eye. Something from the forest, he was sure. Long-limbed and lurching towards the core of the city. Creeping across the buildings as if walking across trees and plants. Climbing on all fours across the doorways and windows and causing damage as it went. Sniffing and searching.

Toad looked at Pip up in the clock workings. 'It's a trick. I told you it was a trick. They're here.' He climbed up to join Pip, where he could hide and look out through the window at the same time.

But it was to Toad and Pip's relief that the creature passed the clock tower by. They took a good long look.

It was a strange thing, slow-moving but somehow terrifying, with long scratching claws and snout, sniffing the cold air. It stopped and turned, looking upwards and around. The boys drew themselves back from the window to avoid being seen and then the beast moved on. It could hear a commotion in the forest, a howl of excitement.

It turned on its heels and sprung into a sprint, heading back to its home to join the frenzy.

Toad took a deep breath. 'Look, Pip, there's nothing here. We should leave it for tonight, get back and get some rest and make sure the others are OK. We can venture out again tomorrow. It's not safe to stay out all night with those things roaming the streets.'

Pip looked downhearted. His head bowed in disappointment.

'You're right, I know. It's just … it's just that … I thought he'd be here.'

'Maybe when the weather's settled he can tell us more. You know, the Captain.'

'OK,' admitted Pip. 'You're right.' He began to climb down from the clock workings. Toad followed him, finding it much harder to squeeze his chubby frame between the steel parts.

They wound their way back through the streets, careful not to bump into any night creatures and listening out for skirmishes that were spilling out into the alleyways here and there. It was a dangerous business – much more so than when they had first ventured out.

Eventually they found their way back to the alleyway that led to the back of the Duprie bakery. The wind had settled a little and it had stopped the cold from biting quite so hard.

Toad walked on ahead as they returned through the tunnelled walkway, but he stopped short when he got to the end.

'What is it?' asked Pip.

Toad didn't say anything. He just raised his arm in the air as if to prevent Pip from coming any further. But Pip couldn't resist and he pushed up to Toad, peering to one side of him. What he saw almost made him cry out in pain and sorrow.

Bark demons. They were emerging from the hole that led to the Duprie basement. Lurching up the staircase and pushing back the hatch with long sinewy limbs, they emerged on to the street. The last to climb out was a hook-handed man in a ragged cloak.

'Oh no!' cried Pip. 'Jarvis!' and his heart thumped so fast he could hardly breathe.

Toad held his hand over Pip's mouth and put a finger to his own lips. 'They'll tear us apart,' he whispered, still holding his hand over Pip, but his friend was gasping so hard that Toad was struggling to restrain him.

'Calm down,' he said. 'I'm not letting go until I know you won't squeal.'

Pip nodded and took deeper, slower breaths, holding his hands up to show his compliance.

'Keep still,' instructed Toad, and they blended into the brickwork of the tunnelled walkway and watched the demons and Jarvis disappear towards the forest.

The boys looked at each other, knowing that they were about to uncover whatever had gone on in the bowels of the bakery basement. What would they find, and how ever would they deal with what was about to come?

CONCERNING WHAT WAS FOUND IN THE BAKERY BASEMENT

The hatch had been left in its open position. It was pitch-black in the basement. Toad crossed the street to a nearby doorway and removed a flaming torch. He returned quickly and headed first down the steps. Pip looked out behind, checking the street for activity before joining him.

The flame of the torch lit up devastation in the room.

The whole place was ransacked, turned completely upside down. Every doorway pulled apart. Every table turned. Every sack of flour ripped to shreds, its white powder choking the whole place up. Everything that was anything reduced to tiny pieces, and not a trace of their brethren to be found.

'They're gone,' said Pip, his eyes wide open with surprise. 'What have they done with them? There was no sign of them when the foresters emerged from here.' He was so exasperated he had to sit himself down in a corner, almost collapsing in a heap with his head in his hands. 'They're not here. For sure they're not here.' Then he jumped up again and carried on turning over tables, pulling out the sacking from the corners, but knowing that he would find nothing.

'They've taken them. They've taken all of them. Even the little ones,' said Pip. 'Poor Frankie. We left her all alone. We left her to those ... those things from the woods, and now look at this. We might never see her again, Toad. Where is she? What do we do?'

'I reckon if we'd been minutes earlier we'd have seen them dragging them away. We'll find them,' said

Toad. He was staring hard around the room, gritting his teeth and curling up his fists. 'And we'll keep on going. Rescuing who we can. We'll build an army and take the forest by storm, that's what we'll do. Surprise them. Show them that we're stronger than they are.'

'This is my fault,' said Pip. 'I left this place. I put us at risk. It's my fault.'

'What's done is done,' said Toad. 'We have to move on for the sake of the others. We can't waste more time. We need to rescue who we can along the way and keep on going.'

Just then a noise interrupted Toad's speech – a clattering from above. A shadow drew across and down the stairs and something peered inside. It was one of the bark demons returning. His moonlike pupils shone into their faces and for a brief moment they all froze at the same time.

And then it came. Like lightning it moved across the floor at them. Toad was waving the flaming torch towards its head and it made a terrible screaming sound that he thought might bring the others. He poked and jabbed at it with the burning wood, but it moved so fast he could barely keep up the pace. It seemed so much stronger than he did.

It pinned him to the floor and when it held him in place it took a good long look at him and sniffed at his scent, filling its nostrils with his Toady smell.

But in its enthusiasm to deal with Toad it had neglected to realize that Pip was right there behind it. Pip knew he would only have one shot and so he had made sure that it was going to be a good one. He stood over the hunched bark demon with his hands shaking, a huge table leg in both hands.

Then, with every ounce of muscle he could muster, he brought the weapon down on his victim, sending it crashing to the ground and falling on top of Toad in the process.

Toad sidled out from underneath the beast and pulled the hatch closed.

THE BIT AT THE END OF CHAPTER EIGHT

It had been a long day for the Captain. Strung at Pip's waist, hanging by a thread and tossed around like a rag. All this running and hiding was wearing him out. While he'd tried to sleep he had sensed a large number of children being discovered and pulled out of their place of safety through a hole.

If Pip and Toad had only thought to ask him, he could have told them exactly where the others were, but in the frenzy, it hadn't occurred to them. And right now, the Captain was tired.

'Leave me alone,' he mumbled. 'The Captain needs his sleep.'

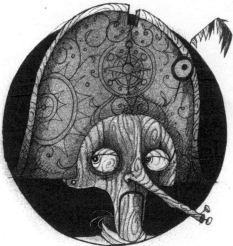

AT WHICH POINT THE CITY IS OVERRUN WITH FORESTERS

There was a war cry from deep within the woods. A cacophony of howls and shrieks that spiralled up into the night like a whirling wind. It was another sign that the forest was about to make more moves on the city.

'Listen,' said Pip. 'Can you hear it? They are coming.'

'We can't stay,' said Toad. 'It's not safe any more.

They will come here first.' He was climbing the steps and peering out through the basement.

'No,' said Pip. 'Not that way.' And he motioned towards the door that led into the bakery shop.

It made sense. They could escape from the top of the house, across the low roofs of the adjoining buildings and head back into the Hollow. Where they'd head they didn't know. But their safety was the first thought. They knew their hiding place would be compromised eventually.

'Wait,' said Pip, stopping on the way up towards the top. 'I've had enough of being frozen out there.' He rifled through piles of clothes in one of the rooms before pulling out a long heavy coat.

Easing into it he put his hands into the long pockets, curling up his fingers and feeling the warmth take away the numbness. It must have belonged to one of the Duprie children at some point. It was too bulky and long for Pip, but the comfort he felt from having it around his shoulders had already made the decision for him. He would not be letting go of it.

'Is there anything for me?' said Toad. 'It will help to disguise us.'

And he picked up a garment that he could barely squeeze into. And then another, and another. He was throwing garments here there and everywhere and trying his best to find something to fit.

CRASH. Something resounded from deep within the basement.

'Just grab something, anything! Quick, they're here!'

It would take those things moments to reach the boys. Toad pulled at something substantial from the pile. It was woollen and heavy and without having a moment to even look at what it was, he had pulled it from the heap. They passed through another door and climbed the stairs into the attic, where a small window would allow them access outside so that they could skitter across the rooftops.

They were tiptoeing now. Trying not to give away that they had headed upwards, and hoping that whatever had burst into the basement had seen that it was empty and headed back outside.

Pip was struggling with the attic window, trying to be as quiet as possible. It was frozen solid and hadn't been opened for some time.

'I need some brute force here,' said Pip. 'Can you—' But he was cut off by a sound from below. A thud came at the door to the attic steps and it sounded as if something was about to burst through.

'Quick!' said Pip. He was still fiddling with the latch and trying to thaw it from its frozen position.

'Here, let me have a look,' said Toad. He picked up a broken chair that lay beneath the window and ploughed it through the frame, sending the whole of the window, glass and frame, out on to the rooftop.

'Ahh, well, I guess that's one way to do it,' admitted Pip.

At that exact moment, the door came through at the bottom of the attic staircase and something came towards them, its heavy breath billowing up the steps.

'Don't let those street urchins out of your sight,' came a familiar voice from below. Jarvis's horrible whining tone was enough to boost the boys into faster action.

'Go!' said Toad and within seconds they were scrambling across the snow-skimmed rooftops of the adjoining buildings. They slipped and slid down the tiles, moving too fast to have any thoughts of being careful.

Behind them in the distance, whatever followed was struggling to squeeze through the gap that was left by the boys' escape, but now the bricks were loosening and it rolled its lumbering bulk on to the tiles.

Jarvis leaned out of the frame after them. 'Come along, little piggies … come to Uncle Jarvis.' His voice came echoing around the chimney stacks.

Toad slipped and was now careering down the tiles uncontrollably. He instinctively grabbed on to Pip and pulled him along. They could see the roof edge coming towards them, but they were helpless. Their feet were scrabbling and their hands and arms were at full stretch to try and stem the speed of the flow. They could only helplessly fall and hope that their landing would be safe.

THUMP! They fell straight on to a facing roof that sat slightly lower than the one they had just come from, their bodies jolting sharply and their newfound woolly garments helping only slightly in taking the impact. And then they continued to slide in the opposite direction down to the bottom of the tiles again, only this time they were able to hang on and dangle precariously from the roof.

Their quick descent had put off their attackers, who were still scrabbling across the first rooftop, finding it hard to get a purchase on the smooth tiles with their clawed digits.

'Quickly!' cried Jarvis, and as he shouted out Pip looked back and saw that something was circling in the distance overhead.

'Witches,' said Toad. 'I don't know how much longer I can hold on.' His face had grown red and he was puffing and panting. Pip's tiny frame was much more agile and he found it easier. There was a window a little further along out of sight. If they edged their way they could climb in and take refuge.

Pip was urging Toad across the roof edge. 'Just keep your grip and shuffle sideways.' He stared across at Toad. He could see that his weight was pulling the guttering away from the edge and if they didn't hurry up they'd be sent crashing into the street below.

'Don't look down,' said Pip. 'Just keep your eyes on me.' And inch by inch he coaxed Toad nearer the window. When they reached it they could allow the ledge to take their weight and the wooden guttering channel creaked as it eased back into place, falling flush with the stone wall.

The noise from below was getting louder and Pip thought that they might have been seen in their lofty position on the roof. Voices came. Official-sounding calls from city folk. Hooves clattered on the stones below.

They could stand comfortably now on the window ledge and across the way they could see the silhouettes of bark demons skittering across the roof. Perhaps it was they who had been seen by the guardsmen. The boys perched inside the recess to remain hidden, out of sight of the creatures' moon eyes.

'Why didn't I think?' said Pip.

'Of what?' asked Toad, his breath gasping.

'To ask the Captain to tell us where they are. Why didn't we remember he was right here?' A grin broke across his face as he pulled the wooden soldier from his waist. 'Tell me, Captain. What did they do to Frankie? Where are the others?' He could not wait a moment longer to find out.

'Into the ovens,' said the Captain and he gave a

sinister cackle. 'A clever idea indeed.'

'Did you hear that?' said Pip. 'Into the ovens. What does that mean?'

'I'm not sure,' said Toad, who was distracted by the demons' escape and unable to think of anything else right now. 'I'll think in a moment, Pip. You know, when we've made sure we're going to get out of this alive. I know it's a small matter, but—'

Pip elbowed the window, knocking the panes through. He had quickly learned from Toad that he should not be so careful when danger is at hand. Toad joined in with his foot and soon the window was demolished, allowing them to hurry inside.

But what happened next was to change everything. Neither of them was sure how it happened. Somehow, as they climbed through the window, Captain Dooley fell from Pip's hands and dropped into the street below.

Horses and men came rushing through the underpass and out into the street, crushing the defenceless wooden soldier into tiny splinters. Only his head remained, rolling into a nearby gutter and landing face down in a frozen pool of ice.

'NO!' cried Pip.

'Shhhh,' said Toad. 'Keep your voice down.' And they stayed still a moment longer as they listened to the bark demons disappearing back the way they had come and Jarvis reprimanding everyone except himself.

'But …'

'Forget it,' said Toad. 'What's done is done.'

AT WHICH POINT THE SEARCH FOR CHILDREN CONTINUES

Pip should have been elated at their escape. But now he was unable to find out whether Frankie and the others were all right. What did 'into the ovens' mean? Now that Captain Dooley was gone, how would they find out, and how would he find his brother?

Another cry from Jarvis could be heard in the distance. 'Don't dare tell me you've lost them again!'

His voice drifted on the wind across the rooftops.

The place was empty – another monument to the city's efforts to strip the city of its residents. It felt almost colder inside than it did out. Pip pulled his long coat closer to his body and felt his way down the steps with the flat of his hand tracing its way down the wall.

Toad was close behind. A half-moon was all that lit the way, its silver paint spilling through the broken window behind them and pouring down the staircase.

The rooms were stripped of furniture. There was nothing anywhere. Just thick dust and fragments of a family's belongings, scattered around like autumn leaves.

'I need to eat,' said Toad. 'I haven't had anything for hours.'

'Here,' said Pip, and he handed him a chunk of bread from his deep pockets.

'Not more bread!' complained Toad. 'I've already eaten two loaves. I'm sick of seeing the stuff.'

'There's nothing else,' said Pip, still feeling his way forward.

A pool of light from a street torch allowed a small moment of respite from the darkness and for a while they sat inside its glow, beneath the window. The panes were frosted and so they were able to scratch out a small viewpoint and look out into the streets for any signs of life.

'If we can reach the drains we can maybe seek out more lost children. I don't fancy our chances against the whole of the forest. Not alone,' said Pip.

'I know,' said Toad. 'I think you're right. We should get down there. See if there are any signs of life.' They knew that it wasn't the distance that would be the problem – it was the hazardous task of passing through the city streets while the dangers of the forest were abroad.

They had ventured through the tunnels before, in Toad's boat. And though it was pitch-black and freezing, it was safe, as long as they knew where they headed. But recently the drain covers had been frozen solid and they had had to make their way everywhere through the streets.

'Whatever we do, we should hold out a while. Jarvis and his crew might still be around here,' added Toad.

'I hope we find the others. Do you think they're all right?' asked Pip.

'I don't know, Pip. I really don't. Frankie knows to use the drains. If they've escaped, there's a slim chance they might be down there.'

Pip's heart fluttered at Toad's optimism. Perhaps he was right.

They stared at each other for a good while. Both of them not really wanting to discuss what they knew could have happened. Both of them thinking of the Captain's last words.

'Sometimes it's best to expect the worst,' said Toad. 'We have to face it. We might never see them again.'

A lump stuck in Pip's throat and he felt the swell of a tear in the corner of his eye.

'Who are you?' came a voice.

The boys peered into the far corner of the room and to their surprise they spied a small girl. She was perhaps a year or two younger than Pip, scruffy and bare-footed, and she emerged from the darkness like a street cat, her dark eyes widening as she stepped into the light.

'Who are *you*?' asked Toad, returning the question.

'My name is Anika.'

'Why are you here?'

'I'm waiting for my brother to return.'

'How long has he been gone?' said Toad.

'Four days. He'll be here soon. His name is Seb. He's one year and two days older than me.'

Pip and Toad gave each other a knowing look.

'Where did he go?' asked Pip.

'To look for food.'

'Did he use the tunnels?'

'No. Seb is afraid of the dark.'

'You can't stay here alone. You might have to come with us. We can try and find your brother,' said Pip.

'No, Pip, we can't. She'll hold us back.' Toad looked hard at him. But in the middle of their argument, Anika stopped them. She had only a small voice but somehow she made herself heard.

'I can't move from here,' she said bluntly.

The boys stopped their talking, turned to her and listened.

'Why?' asked Pip.

'Because of Bunny.'

'Who is Bunny?' asked Toad and Pip at the same time.

Anika stepped out of the light and pointed to something in the corner. Behind her, lying on a mound of cloth and old sacking, was another child. As they approached they saw that it was another boy and that he was sick. His face was filthy and his hair, like hers, was long and unkempt. He was sleeping and his breathing was erratic. He needed help, and quick.

'When did you last eat anything?' asked Toad.

'I don't know. Maybe a week ago,' she said.

Toad took out his bread and handed it to her. Then he walked to the window. He was gathering his bearings, working out where they were in the city so that he might remember who was nearby that could help. He knew that they were not too far from Percival Floyd's, but not too long ago they had sought refuge with him and he had got into trouble. It was unlikely he would help and probably unfair to ask for his assistance again.

Pip was staring at the boy in the corner. He felt helpless, and even in the dim half-light the child looked desperately sick. He took the last of the bread from his pocket and made small crumbs to feed him, sharing the rest with the girl. She gulped the bread down without making any attempt to chew it.

'I won't be long,' said Toad and he took a good last look from the window before he made his way to the door.

'No,' said Pip. 'Not on your own. I'm not losing you as well.'

'I'll not be long,' said Toad, holding his hands out in a calming gesture. 'You stay here.'

And before Pip could argue, he was gone, out into the night.

A feeling came over Pip that he had not had since he had first arrived alone in the Hollow. A feeling of complete emptiness. He had not been away from Toad and Frankie for some time, and if things didn't work out, he might now lose the pair of them.

He turned to look at the others. Anika was staring at him.

'Has he gone to bring Seb back?'

'I think he's gone to see what he can find to eat,' said Pip.

'Would you like some water?' she asked him.

'You have water?'

She didn't speak. Instead she took him to a small wooden bucket in the middle of the next room that caught drips of water from a leak up above. Pip dipped his hands into the freezing shallow pool and poured it between his lips.

Only minutes had passed, and Pip felt as if he was counting every second. As the time went by he grew more and more anxious, parading up and down the darkened staircase to peek out of all the windows to look for any sign of Toad.

Something passed outside in the street. Voices, shouting, the clattering of hooves again. He watched through the window from a distance. It was a clash of forest and city. One of those long-snouted creatures had turned the corner into the path of an oncoming group of guardsmen who were on the lookout for revenge. An earlier attack on the city had left their brethren dead upon the street. Pip turned. He could not look. He only heard the sound of the creature squealing and listened to a crunch of bones against the doorway. He spent the next few moments in silent stillness, holding back in the darkness with the little ones, waiting for the activity to subside.

He crouched in a corner, and after quite some time he felt his eyes closing and at length he nodded off.

A noise from the back of the house woke him. A door rattling. Had they been seen? Were the woodsfolk or the guards working their way inside?

Pip opened his eyes to see Anika jumping to her feet, the whites of her eyes piercing through the shadows.

How would they move the boy they called Bunny?

Where could they head and not be seen?

'I'm here.'

It was Toad. He was carrying something and grinning to himself.

'Right, get stuck into that.' He placed a container on the ground and began to pull more bread from the pockets of his new coat.

'Where did you g—'

'Don't ask,' said Toad, interrupting. 'Just eat.'

WHICH EXPLAINS A THING OR TWO ABOUT THE ESCAPEES

Pip had boiled the water that had collected in the wooden bucket. He had made a small fire on the stone tiles in the middle of the room, explaining to the others that if they used the fireplace the chimney would smoke and attract attention. He then gave the boiled water to Toad, who was going to carry it to the nearest drain cover and rinse it around the rim to release the ice.

'Sounds easy,' said Toad.

'We'll be fine,' insisted Pip. 'I'll go on ahead and make sure it's clear, and you follow.' He turned to Anika. 'You have to sit tight, just like you have been doing. Don't move. Don't leave the house. Keep out of the light and we'll be back soon with more help.'

'OK,' she agreed, but she didn't want them to leave. Bunny was fast asleep and when they left she ran to the window against their advice and watched them disappear around the corner.

When the streets and alleyways are filled with nightmare creatures and at every other turn you will find a guardsman on horseback or a demon in search of children, each journey through the Hollow is always much too far. And so it was with great concern that Pip and Toad left the house they had found and headed off with the intention of finding an entrance to the drains. Especially when they had made an absolute promise to return as quickly as possible.

The catacombs are dark and even colder than the streets above, and when the temperatures are extreme the drain covers are frozen solid and access is poor. Both Pip and Toad were determined to get into the tunnels that ran under the city and find Frankie and the others. Once they were in, nothing would come down there. The authorities didn't know that the children used them and the foresters disliked the water and wouldn't venture near.

The silhouettes of the two boys were momentarily picked out by the white landscape of the city. They would have to be quick before they were noticed. Pip poured the container of water around the rim of a drain cover and Toad quickly forced a stick under it as steam billowed upwards, causing his eyes to water.

'We're in,' he said as the rounded hatch eased away from the ice. Their bodies disappeared downwards and the cover was pulled back across the hole.

It was some time since Toad had first brought Pip into the twists and turns of brickwork that ran beneath the city. The water flowed through the maze of winding bends down here in much the same way as the river flowed through the city. It carried the water from the drains and, when it was necessary, the overflow from the river.

When they got there, to their surprise, the waterway was completely frozen. Toad had never known it cold enough to do so. But it was easier – it meant that they could walk across it and not have to worry about finding one of the small boats that were scattered around the tunnels.

They skated across the ice with a meagre torch to light their way. Toad roughly mapped out a journey that would ensure a good search of a large section of the Hollow. They would head out towards the Duprie bakery.

Their feet made strange echoes as they trod across the ice. They could not see far ahead, the torch only seeming to allow them a shallow vision of what lay to the fore.

Up ahead they found something that made them stop

a while. At their feet was what looked like children's belongings – a small shawl or blanket, and a clothes peg painted with a face and costume that probably served as some poor child's doll. They looked as if they had been dropped along the way. Pip took the wooden peg in his hand and inspected the face. It was carefully drawn, with a smile and two red rounded dots for the cheeks. One side of the peg was splintered, but the rest was intact. He smiled and placed it in his pocket.

'To know of more children on the move is good,' said Toad. 'Let's push on.'

Pip called out, sending a 'hello' rattling through the curved brick route of the catacombs, but nothing came back except his own echo.

Up ahead the whole space widened out in front of them, forming an impressive arc of brickwork above and a broad circular vista of ice below. Large icicles hung from the overflow inlets above and the echoes of their voices changed in tone.

'We're right in the middle of the city,' announced Pip.

'Well done,' said Toad proudly. 'Your knowledge is improving.'

'Beneath the square,' Pip continued. 'Where the fountain sits.'

'That's it. The Duprie bakery is just a little further,' said Toad. 'We're not far from the authority quarters.'

So they ventured onwards and kept a lookout for lost companions.

Pip grew almost excited by the prospect of finding others. He imagined their faces. Perhaps they were gathered together in small armies, in which case there would be many of them. He was sure that Billy would be there too, waiting for him. Perhaps he had heard by now that a boy called Eddie Pipkin was in the Hollow and had come to rescue the others with his friend Toad. If he did, he'd know to expect his own long-lost brother. Pip's heart drummed faster at the thought of their meeting.

Up ahead was a vague, misty kind of light that spelled the way into the drains from the keep.

The huge iron grate was pulled to one side.

'Strange,' said Toad. 'These drains lead to the city prison. That huge iron grate stops anything getting out.'

'Or in?' said Pip.

'Well, yes, I guess so. Let's take a look,' Toad suggested, and so they clambered up the slippery drain hole to see if they could get near to the city jail.

It was all too easy. There were no sounds, just an echoey silence that spelled an emptiness. They drew closer, finding themselves inside the stone-cold walls of the prison. Its doors open, its rooms emptied of life. Odd shoes, bits of broken toys, small hats and scattered garments. Remains of what used to be there, surrounded by a dull, cold silence.

They braved a little further.

The stone keep lay deprived of its captured children. There were ragged remains of torn and tattered clothing on the bricks and iron bars, as if some struggle had ensued. Had the children met their end at the hands of the forest creatures?

'Surely not,' said Toad. 'They would never venture down here. They hate the water.'

'But it's frozen,' said Pip. 'They have nothing to fear.'

'I didn't think of that,' admitted Toad. 'Perhaps you're right. Maybe they were here.'

Further investigation only served to prove the point.

The whole place was empty of its prisoners and not a trace of anyone was left, save for a second wooden clothes peg with a painted face and costume, and a single shoe. Pip's heart sank as he picked up the peg doll and tucked it into his pocket. His hopes of finding his brother and Frankie and the others were dwindling even further.

They were not far from the bakery now and it seemed a good idea to complete the journey and make sure they could find no one else. They emerged from the bowels of the city keep and returned to the brickwork tunnels.

'This way,' urged Toad, edging round a corner into deeper darkness. Pip followed on, holding the still flaming torch aloft to create some light, and they moved on in silence, listening to their echoing footsteps.

In a short while they had made the distance to where the bakery stood. As expected there was nothing to speak of.

'Hang on,' said Pip. 'What's that up ahead?' They moved along and Pip created another pool of light with the torch, highlighting a couple of large steel discs.

'What's that?' Toad asked.

'The vent outlets from the ovens!' exclaimed Pip. 'They've pushed their way out. The Captain was right. A clever idea indeed, he said.'

'What?' said Toad.

'Into the ovens. That's what the Captain said. Remember? It's Frankie and the others. They've escaped through the ovens and come out through the vents into the drains. They must be here.' A huge smile broke across Pip's face.

'I hope you're right,' said Toad, smiling. It was the best news they could have possibly had. It gave them hope.

'We should carry on. We'll get to them eventually,' insisted Pip. 'They can't have gone too far.'

'Hold on,' said Toad, raising his hands. 'We need to be careful. That's enough searching for now. It would take us all night to search the catacombs from beginning to end. There are only two children that we know the whereabouts of for sure. And we should get back to them. They need us.'

Pip knew Toad was right. Bunny and Anika were in great danger.

Toad stared into the darkness. He was plotting the route back through the drains. 'It will take us a good while to return,' he said. 'But they'll be wondering where we are right now, and the boy needs help.'

They turned and walked into the maze of brickwork and Pip waved his dash of light into the black to unveil the way forward. With their newfound optimism that Frankie was alive and well and that others were on the move, they made their way back.

WHICH REVEALS A LITTLE MORE ABOUT THE INN

Jarvis was taking his frustration out on the streets. He was still reeling from the previous escapade of losing track of the boys and had ordered attacks on the houses he knew to be occupied.

The noise and disturbance was echoing down to Pip and Toad in the depths of the drains. The return to the little ones promised to be a long one. Witches clung like

bats to the rooftops and the skies were filled with life.
No matter where they tried to come up, the drain covers
were always in the wrong place as the forest seemed to
be bringing ever increasing numbers into the alleyways.

'The plan is working,' grinned Jarvis, who was back
in the depths of the forest, furiously firing his orders.
'The city guards are emerging on their horses to take
control of the streets. The locals are pulling together in
large groups. They haven't a chance. We'll destroy
them. Don't forget, I want those little rats and I want
them now,' he roared.

Two crows landed on a nearby post. It was Esther
and Silas, companions of the woodsfolk.

'Well?' said Jarvis. 'Any more luck?'

'Not yet, sire,' squawked Silas.

'Keep looking. And don't come back to me until you
have news!'

The crows returned to the air and soared away
through the covered alleyways.

Beneath those very streets the dilemma continued.

'There is one thing we can do,' said Pip.

'What's that?' asked Toad, looking dejected.

'We could return to the inn and seek help from your father. He would have word that you are safe, and we could nurse the sick boy in safety.'

Toad looked hard at Pip. He had not considered going back to the Deadman's Hand. He had not seen his father for some time and the thought of walking through his door and surprising him filled him with excitement. He thought of the look on his father's face. But would they be welcomed when they brought so much trouble? Jarvis had already attempted to burn down the inn.

'Surely the inn is safe by now,' said Pip. 'It is quite some time ago that Jarvis discovered we were there.'

'And the war between forest and city is keeping him occupied,' added Toad, as if to reassure himself. 'They won't be looking for us now, they are busy sharpening their weapons and waging battle on the streets.'

'Let's return to Anika and Bunny and take them to safety,' said Pip, and Toad nodded in agreement.

It was a struggle to coax Anika and the boy into the underground journey. Anika insisted that Seb would be returning and Bunny was barely able to walk unaided. They wrapped him in sheets and sacking to keep him warm and pulled him along the ice on a makeshift sledge made from broken door timbers and old rope. Anika was without any kind of footwear and she had to bind her feet in rags.

It was cold, but Pip and Toad sweated profusely with the effort and Anika dragged on behind them. In places the ice was thin and the extra weight made for nervous moments on the frozen waterway. Again they found signs of children – this time a woollen hat. They tried calling out again, but nothing came back in return.

After following a series of twists and turns through

the maze of tunnels for some considerable time, Pip spied Toad's little rowing boat up ahead, signalling that they had reached the access point to the cellar of the Deadman's Hand. The boat was sealed into its place by the ice and hadn't moved for some time.

They climbed the steps that led to the drain cover and popped their heads up into the cellar of the inn.

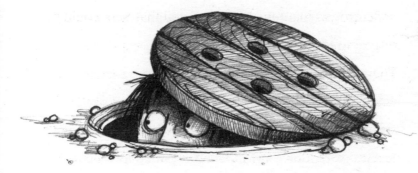

It felt strange to return and Toad was eager to head up inside and sit by the fire to join his father. There was always food and drink and warmth at the inn.

The basement felt cold. It was dark and empty. They pulled Bunny up through the rounded hole and laid him down again. Pip lit a handful of candles from the store and made a comfortable space for Anika and Bunny to wait. They would fetch Sam and he could carry the boy up into the house.

Toad and Pip raced up the stairs to the main room at the inn. All was in darkness. The room was empty of life and it was as cold in here as it would be outside. Toad walked into the middle of the room and kneeled down by the fire, digging his hands into the ash and blackened embers.

'This fire hasn't been alight for some time,' he said, turning to his companion.

Pip stared around the room, holding up the torch. It had been turned over. There were bottles and barrels smashed into pieces, piles of broken furniture, and the doorways into the rooms had been pulled awkwardly from the frames.

'He's not here, Pip,' said Toad. 'Something's happened. He's been taken.'

Pip had never seen him look so crestfallen. In the orange light of the torch his saddened face said everything. The foresters had been here, they had turned the whole place over and Sam would be locked up in some dismal hole. Perhaps in a part of the keep in the city or perhaps at the undergate in the forest. Both were as bad.

Pip went to the window. He pulled back the shutters, expecting to see the view of the Hollow that he was familiar with, but the windows had been boarded-up from the outside. He went to the door and found the same issue.

Outside there was more noise again. Some skirmish between city and forest, but they could not see.

'This will be our fortress,' declared Pip. 'We'll build an army from here. And when we're ready, we'll take back the city from the forest.'

And at that, they returned to the cellar and took the newcomers to the secret annexe where Pip, Toad and Frankie had once hidden safely.

REGARDING A SMALL SURPRISE

At least at the inn, they had access to food. Despite the ransacking, much of the supplies had remained untouched. They hoped that with food and warmth and good care, Bunny would soon be back to full strength.

The annexe was just as they had left it. But it was so well disguised that it was unlikely anyone would ever find it unless they knew where to look.

The sick boy was sitting up in bed and Anika was taking a bowl of warm water to mop his face. He was filthy and ragged, almost feral, with wild-looking long hair and a muddy complexion.

He hadn't spoken yet. He only managed to murmur now and then to confirm that he had eaten enough or that he was comfortable. They were still not sure that he knew exactly what was going on.

Toad was staring through the spyglass at the top of the ladder and Pip was taking a good long look at the sick boy. It was the first time he had even looked at his face. They had spent so much time in darkness that it was only now that he was really able to see him.

'Why do they call you Bunny?' asked Pip.

The boy looked at Pip and a tiny smile came across his face.

'Why is he grinning?' said Pip, turning to Anika.

'He's not,' she said, wiping the dirt from his brow. 'He's showing you his teeth.'

And then Pip noticed the slightly goofy look that Bunny had. How his strong white teeth stood slightly proud of his mouth and showed themselves in an almost rabbit-like way.

'Oh, I see,' said Pip with a giggle. 'What's his real name?'

'I don't know,' said Anika. 'It was Seb who named him. We found him in the street before we hid in the place you found us.'

Anika continued to clean the boy's face and as she did he began to look somehow familiar to Pip. After she'd brushed his hair she tucked him into his bed as if he was a replacement for her favourite doll.

'My name ... is ... Billy ...' said the feral boy, '... Billy Pipkin,' opening his mouth for the first time before closing his eyes and falling asleep once more.

Toad looked round immediately, the shock almost knocking him from his lofty position on the ladder. Pip stared wide-eyed and open-mouthed, unable to utter a word. His eyes bulging in his head, he turned to Toad, who by now had fallen from the ladder in surprise and crashed into a heap of wooden boxes.

'Did you hear that?' said Pip as a huge grin broke across his face. 'It's Billy!' He held the candle up to his face to take a closer look in the darkness.

'Billy, it's me, Eddie,' said Pip. He had no notion of whether Billy knew of his existence or not. It seemed that for now, he wouldn't find out. Poor Billy was exhausted and Pip was unable to waken him.

'Better let him sleep,' said Toad, who now stood over Billy, looking between him and Pip and suddenly taking in the likeness between them. 'It's really him, Pip,' he grinned. 'But it looks like all that travelling has worn him out.'

Pip was unable to contain himself – so much so that he almost put them at risk. He leaped up, parading around, and then he sat slumped in a chair, as if knocked out by the news. Then he ran around the place whooping and hollering at the top of his voice.

'Quiet!' pleaded Toad. 'You'll wake the whole forest.'

'I don't understand,' said Anika, after Pip had given her half an explanation. 'Bunny is … your brother?'

'Yes, I think so,' said Pip.

'You think so? How could you not know?' she asked.

'Well,' said Pip, 'it's a long story.' He was so full of excitement that he started to tell the whole tale right from the very beginning – his escape from the orphanage and arrival in the Hollow, and that he knew nothing of his family or from where he came.

And if he had taken a moment to look, he would have realized that young Anika was asleep well before he got to the end and so there he was, in the half-light, explaining his story to nobody but his excited little self.

'And so that's how I found that Billy was here,' said Pip, reaching the end of the story. 'Toad thought that the Captain might be tricking me, didn't you, Toad?

'Yes, I admit it. I didn't trust the Captain. But he was right, Pip. You were right.'

Toad turned over and his head sank into his pillow as he closed his eyes. Anika did the same, her mop of hair disappearing under the sheets as she curled up to gather warmth.

'How can they sleep?' said Pip to himself. 'How can they possibly even think of closing their eyes? The most amazing thing that could ever possibly happen has just happened and they're all asleep.'

He leaned over his newfound sibling and held the torch close, making himself comfortable by his side.

'Can you hear me, Billy? Are you OK? Billy … are you asleep?'

He waited and then he asked again. 'Billy, it's me. It's Pip, your brother. Are you OK?'

'Billy is OK,' came his reply, but he was responding from a deep sleep.

'If you need anything, Billy, just wake me … OK, Billy? I'll speak to you soon … in the morning.'

'Pip, can you just go to sleep?'

'Sorry, Toad, I'm sorry.'

'It's OK, Pip, it's OK. Just go to sleep.'

'I will, I promise, I'll go to sleep. Goodnight, Toad.'

'Yes … goodnight.'

CONCERNING A KNOCK AT THE DOOR

It was almost dawn when it happened, but it was still dark. Pip had taken some time settling into sleep, and when he finally did, exhaustion sent him into a deep slumber. But it was a peaceful rest that he was to be pulled out of abruptly.

A bang at the door came from downstairs. It came once, twice, three times before it woke Pip and Toad.

'What was that?' said Toad, sitting up and rubbing his eyes.

'It's the door!' said Pip.

The others were still sleeping. 'Come on,' said Toad, standing up. Pip was already on his feet and at the door with something in his hand to use as a weapon should the need arise. They descended the steps in seconds. As they reached the ground floor the banging came again, but harder, and now something was pulling at the frame.

'Wait,' said Pip, holding Toad back and watching the door being yanked from its position. They crept closer and listened to what came from the other side.

'What is it?' asked Toad.

'Voices,' said Pip.

'Yes, I know that. Whose voices?'

'Children's voices.'

'Children?' said Toad.

'Just open the door … quickly, before we're seen!' came a shout from outside.

But Pip was rattling the shutters open and drawing their attention, frantically urging them to go to the side door in the darkened alleyway. A procession of children – twenty, maybe thirty or more – rushed through the drifts that ran up against the walls of the alleyway, heading towards the door like a pack of animals.

One by one they passed through the door, shaking their coats and kicking the snow from their boots. And at the back, the very last one, with a shawl around her shoulders and draped half across her face, was Frankie. Breathing heavily from exhaustion and unable to utter a word, she was pulled inside by the boys. Pip was astonished and pleased all at the same time.

'It's you! It's really you!' cried Pip, hugging Frankie.

'With a small army,' said Toad, looking around him at the sea of reddened faces, huddled together and looking happy to be inside.

'There is more good news,' gasped Pip. 'I have found my brother. He is upstairs taking rest.'

Frankie turned to Toad, open-mouthed in disbelief.

'He's right,' said Toad. 'Go take a look for yourself.'

'But … I can't believe it's true,' she admitted. 'Where did you find him?'

'It's a long tale,' insisted Pip. 'We'll tell you everything.'

There were many faces, all new to Toad and Pip.

'Where have you come from?' asked Pip, turning to a group of two boys and two girls.

'We were hiding out in a disused house, and the foresters came, but we managed to escape into the catacombs,' explained one boy, pointing out the two girls as his original companions.

'And they bumped into me,' explained the second. 'I had come from the Duprie bakery. I found it open and deserted and hoped to find food, but the place was attracting attention so I headed elsewhere.'

'Who are you?' Pip questioned further.

'My name is Sebastian. I need to return to the city. My sister is alone with a sick boy that we helped. I must get back and take them food. Can you help?'

A smile broke across Pip's face.

'You're Seb?'

The boy nodded.

'You don't need to go anywhere,' announced Toad. 'They're here with us. We're all safe.'

'You mean my sister is here, with you?'

'Yes, Anika. That's how we knew who you were. She's here, with the boy you called Bunny. He is my brother,' said Pip proudly, 'and I must thank you for saving him. They are asleep upstairs right now. Come and greet them.'

Relief broke across Seb's face.

'And the rest of you?'

'We escaped through the backs of the ovens through the vents and out to the drains,' explained Frankie. 'We spent several nights down there in the cold. We had to move eventually and when we found the drain from the city keep we managed to loosen the fixings and take out the grate. We headed in and released the others. The next night we came up into the city and when we knew that you were here we set off this way.'

'How did you know we were here?' questioned Pip.

Frankie raised her eyebrow with a knowing look. She put her hand inside her shawl and pulled out the broken effigy of Captain Dooley.

'He has his uses,' admitted Frankie. 'We found him, face down in the street. He still … speaks. But only just.'

'He's freaky. I don't like him,' said one of the small boys and he turned away, crying, so as not to have to look at him.

Pip took hold of the Captain, holding him by the head. His body was cracked and gnarled into an unrecognizable shape, and only his head was intact.

Pip took him to one side and inspected the damage, holding him carefully under the torchlight. His heavy head held on to the tattered remains of his pathetic little body.

'Thank you, Captain,' he said. 'You helped me find my brother. If it hadn't been for you, I might never have known who he was.'

The Captain made a short croaking sound, as if trying to speak. His heavy eyelids closed and he fell into a deep sleep.

'There is something you must know,' said Frankie, and she beckoned Toad forward so that he might be in hearing distance.

'What is it?' said Pip.

'There are more children. In the catacombs. They await good news. They're ready to fight if they need to.'

'How many?' asked Toad.

'A hundred, maybe more! We couldn't all move at once.'

'That's good. We need power in numbers,' said Pip.

'There's something else,' said Frankie. 'We … lost someone.'

'You lost someone?'

'Yes … a small girl. She'd carried a handful of small wooden peg dolls, painted with faces and costumes. When we hit the streets she realized she'd lost two. She was hysterical, screaming and frantic. She set off running back to where we'd come from. I tried to warn her but—'

'It's OK,' said Pip, wrapping his arms around her and letting her cry into his shoulder.

'She was only tiny, she knew no better.'

'It's OK. You did well, Frankie. You've saved so many.'

'I could have stopped her,' she sobbed, 'I could have saved one more.'

There was nothing Pip could say to soothe her. Instead he let her cry and cry until she had nothing left inside.

'Come on,' said Toad. 'There are enough of us now. We can win this war.'

A smile broke across the boys' faces. 'Let's settle everybody upstairs,' suggested Pip, 'and then we can sit and put a plan into place. We can make this work,' he insisted. 'I have an idea.'

They herded the children up to the first floor and followed on behind. When the children were in place and comfortable Pip took hold of the Captain again. He placed him on a shelf next to Toad's books and odds and ends, making sure he was comfortable. And then for the second time he thanked him for all he'd done.

A WORD AT THE END OF CHAPTER FOURTEEN

'A cosy hideout for sure,' said Esther, pulling out her wings to stabilize herself as she shuffled across the ledge. 'How many?'

'There must have been more than twenty children moving across the city to get to the inn. And I guess there are more inside. I would think we have a large hideout on our hands,' informed Silas.

The two crows were perched across from the tavern, sharing warmth from each other in the crumbling stone recess of an old arched window. It was better to work in twos, they had found. And here

was a perfect example of their success. They should head back to the forest now and tell the others. It was time for their brothers and sisters to make their claim on the Deadman's Hand. And then of course they could take the rest of the city by storm.

They opened their black wings in unison and lifted themselves upwards into the breeze, drifting towards the trees.

A WORD
BEFORE
CHAPTER
FIFTEEN

The children sat together in a large group. Food was passed around – bread broken and shared, containers of water filled and emptied.

Pip was sharing his thoughts with Billy. Quizzing him about his past and trying to get to the bottom of where he had come from while Frankie and Toad took care of the little ones.

'It almost seems too much of a coincidence that you happened to be right here, in the Hollow,' said Pip.

'I don't know what you mean,' said Billy.

'Well, I came from a long way away to a wild and remote city, and when I discovered I had a twin brother he turned out to be just around the corner. It hardly makes sense,' explained Pip.

'You don't know much, do you, Pip?' answered Billy, grinning.

'Eh?'

'When we were born our parents were unable to take care of us. Our mother became ill, our father could not look after us and work at the same time. I was left with a young couple who were only able to look after one more child and so you were sent away to an orphanage.'

'But where was this place? The place where we were born?'

Bunny smiled and his little white rabbit's teeth stood proud as he broke into a giggle. 'You still don't get it, Pip, do you? We were born here, in Hangman's Hollow. This place is where you came from. I've never been outside of these walls.

When you escaped and came here
you never realized that you were
coming home.'

'You mean, I'm from here,
like Frankie and Toad?'

'Of course.' Billy grinned, his
white teeth showing just a little more
as he raised a laugh.

And from that moment Pip knew
he would never quite feel the same
again.

'Right,' said Toad, sitting at
Pip's side with Frankie. 'About
this plan …'

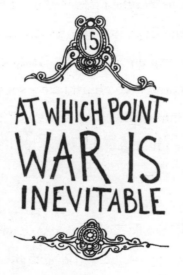

AT WHICH POINT WAR IS INEVITABLE

Nothing causes quite as much excitement in the forest as a sighting of children. Especially in healthy numbers.

'To know the whereabouts of the most vulnerable ones in the city is to know its weakest point,' Jarvis explained to an assembly of the Stone Circle.

Silas and Esther sat proudly perched on a rotted trunk. They had shown that their teamwork had paid off.

'When night falls again, we shall head to the Deadman's Hand and make light work of the pickings,' Jarvis continued. 'It will not be difficult. The place has been emptied and is a refuge for the children. Sleep well, woodlings, for the night will need your strength. This will be the final push into the city and soon we will have our grip on Hangman's Hollow. Stixx, when the moment is right, you must take a snoop and make sure that the inn is filled with children. I am determined that our plans will not be thwarted this time. Silas, fly with her.'

'Very well,' she said.

'And don't be seen. We need to take them by surprise.'

Howls came spiralling up through the frozen forest. The black shapes of witches circled above in great numbers, stirring up the clouds with their silhouettes, and the promise of change filled the forest with excitement.

Only a stone's throw away from where the woodsfolk slept heartily in preparation, the city was readying itself for more confrontation as night fell. Adults from the city prison were given weapons and armour and instructed on how to fight. Most of them were speechless and terrified at the prospect of having to battle for their right to remain in the city. But come what may, they would soon be out on the streets. There was no choice.

One man turned to another, a big fellow by his side. Perhaps someone so powerful was a good person to know right now. The man introduced himself and they swore that they would look out for each other.

'My name is Leo,' said the first. 'I am just a humble shoemaker but I harboured my brother's children in my

house. I was imprisoned a long time ago. I have grown older and weaker, but now I am faced with fighting a war.'

'I have seen you before, I think,' said the big man. 'Perhaps you came and drank at my tavern. My name is Sam and I am landlord at the Deadman's Hand on the other side of town. I too harboured children – my son and his friends – and so now I am here, among my neighbours and imprisoned for nothing. None of us have done any wrong. If taking care of your own kind and having compassion for your fellow man is a crime, then let me hang at the gallows.'

The city mayor Hector Stubbs had overheard Sam. He knew it was time to make things clear before the battle began. 'Listen, people,' he pleaded, 'lend me your attention for a moment. You have been imprisoned with your fellow men, for harbouring children against the will of the city. But if you want the freedom to live here with your families, you need to join together with my armed guards and battle against the force of the forest. If we can overcome the foresters, we shall live in peace and children can return to the Hollow.'

'Where are the children from your prison?' asked Sam. 'You have kept us here within your walls, unable to see our own kin. You swore that they were held here, like us, yet there is no sign of them.'

'I'm afraid the children's quarters have been emptied,' replied Stubbs.

'Emptied?'

'The iron grate that runs into the drains was removed and the children are missing. There is no word of them. I'm afraid that for now, we must fear the worst.' Hector paused. 'Let us hope that you get to those forest folk before they get to your children.'

Sam's heart sank. The last he had heard of Toad and the others, they were on the run, fleeing from Floyd's place after Jarvis had chanced upon them. Who knew whether they had ended up in the hands of the forest or the city prisons, or indeed if they had escaped back into the houses of the Hollow?

'But what about my boy?' begged Sam. 'Was he here, in your prison?'

It was too late. Hector Stubbs had passed them by and suddenly the crowd was shifting forward. A steel gate lifted ahead of them. The sound of rusted chains clunking over and over accompanied the raising of the iron criss-crossed frame used to hold the prisoners in the keep. It was time to leave the confines of incarceration and head for the streets.

Hundreds of feet took their first move forward and

stepped out into the night, not knowing if they would ever see daylight again.

The forest was stirring again, its evil and hungry children wakening to the dark hours. They would soon gather at the Deadman's Hand. Digging their claws into the crisp cold earth, they headed onwards. The witches took to the air and circled, finding their bearings before homing in on the city tavern. They would roost at the chimney tops until the rest of the woodsfolk were able to reach them and they could join forces.

WHEN THE INN
RECEIVES
A VISITOR

The children were assembled upstairs at the inn.
That way, they had warning if someone entered the
premises.

'There is a lot of activity out there,' said Toad. He
could see the tops of the forest trees bubbling with
movement and hear calls and shrieks surrounding
the city.

They had been sitting with a pile of food scraps, sharing out the crumbs, patting their bellies and blowing hard. It was not easy to feed so many hungry mouths, but they had managed it.

'I couldn't eat a single thing more,' said Pip.

'You can always eat more,' argued Toad, turning his attention from the gap in the window to the assembled group.

Pip chuckled and Billy stared at him in disbelief. Anika took little notice. She pointed out that they were without water and headed downstairs with the empty bucket.

'She shouldn't be alone,' said Pip and he jumped up and followed on behind her. Seb followed in a bid to be helpful. 'You stay there, Billy,' Pip said, instructing his brother to stay in his bed. If something happened, he was not yet ready for any kind of confrontation.

The boys waited in the tavern bar. Pip stood by the hearth and thought how great it would be to light the fire. He imagined the roaring flames and he could almost feel the blistering heat brushing up against his face. He remembered the warm nights, sat with Frankie and Toad, listening to Sam's stories, and for a moment he was lost in thought.

Then Anika appeared from the scullery where the water barrel was kept, waddling along with the bucket full to the brim, and now she stood between him and the fire. She stared closely at him and blew in his face to bring him out from his trance. Pip jumped and took a step back, bringing himself to his senses, realizing that she was waiting for them with the heavy bucket.

Pip had constantly been surprised by Anika's strength but until now he hadn't said anything. 'You can lift to say you're so little,' he said, smiling at her.

'Oh, shut up, Pip,' she answered and he immediately saw he'd offended her. 'Just cos I'm a girl, doesn't mean I 'aven't got muscles.' She held the bucket in one hand and flexed her right bicep, grinning from ear to ear.

Seb laughed. 'Careful, Pip. She's a feisty one.'

But the moment was broken with a disturbance. A tapping and scuttling sound came from the chimney breast. Pip stared upwards and Anika turned round so that all three of them faced the fireplace. The noise grew. Small chips of stone rattled down the chimney breast and a scratching, scraping noise announced that something was stuck in there.

'It's a bird,' said Anika and she placed the bucket on the floor and moved forward.

'No,' said Pip and he pulled on her arm to hold her back without taking his eye from the chimney.

A shabby black lump emerged from the chimney breast and landed in the blackened coals. 'Ahh, drat,' came a whiney nasal voice and it got to its feet. It was shaking itself off, batting the dust from its shroud and then it spied them. The children stared at the old hag, not daring to move.

At first she appeared almost frightened, but when she saw how alarmed they were, she regained her confidence.

'Well, well, well … what have we here? Children of men. How peculiar.' She grinned and ran a scratchety long-fingered nail around Pip's chin, eycing him closely.

'Who … who are you?' asked Pip nervously.

'I'll ask the questions,' said the old hag. And then something fluttered down the chimney breast behind her. It was a crow and it stood in the hearth for a moment before it flew to settle on the woman's shoulder, cocking its head to one side and looking quizzically at the small ones.

'You weren't supposed to be seen,' said the bird, whispering in her ear.

'Never mind, eh! Don't tell the others. Good work, Silas,' said the old woman. 'Very good work indeed.' And from what she said, Pip surmised that the crow had spotted their movement at the inn.

Toad clattered down the steps and held his torch out into the room. 'What on earth are you three playing at,

you've been age—' He stopped in his tracks.

'Oooh, a fat one. He will make a good stew,' the witch started.

But as she turned to look at Toad, Pip lifted the bucket from the floor and threw the water over her in panic.

They would have never guessed in a million years that it would have had the effect that it did. The witch recoiled in horror, her skin in blistering pain, and the children stepped back, terrified. Her crooked frame pulled the cloak around itself. Smoke and steam and a horrible stench filled the air and then the hag turned on her heels, squealing, and scrabbled her way back up inside the brickwork. The bird turned and fled, cawing loudly and escaping after her.

'Light the fire,' said Pip.

Anika protested, 'But I thought you said—'

'They know we're here,' said Pip. 'There's no going back now. We're going headlong into all-out warfare. We need to be armed and ready. They will be here, and soon. We should bring more water. If it is so effective against the wood witch, it must be our weapon. All of us need to be ready for war. Our plan has to be put into place, and sooner than we thought.'

Pip called out to Frankie, and when she came running he told her that it was time to leave. She gathered herself together and they headed for the cellar, where they would take to the drains.

Throwing logs into the grate of the fire, Toad placed his torch at their centre until they caught light and smoke and flames went billowing up the chimney breast.

It was a sign to the city. A sign that announced that the children's army was ready for war.

AT WHICH POINT BLOOD IS SPILLED

Clawed feet were marching towards the Deadman's Hand. A procession of beasts made their way, some on two legs and some on four, some more familiar to the city than others. Roach gave himself away among the crowd with the strange gait to his walk and the insectoid-like movement of his six limbs. The inn sits close to the

135

forest. It is a large building and easy to find, its height helping to show itself from a distance, and now that the huge fire was lit downstairs, smoke was clouding up into the night, as if to entice the creatures along.

But no wood-going creature would attempt the chimney while fire burned below. The fire and smoke would at least prevent those beasts from entering through the scorching flue.

Now just when those creatures had their eyes on the children at the tavern and all else seemed to be unimportant, something was about to step in the way.

'I can hear noise approaching,' said Leo, turning and looking up at Sam as they marched.

'I hear it too,' Sam replied. 'I would know the sound of the forest anywhere.' Feeling his heart beat a little faster, he gripped his weapon harder and gritted his teeth.

'Stay near me,' he said.

The route from the forest to the Deadman's Hand cuts by the authority buildings and so it was inevitable that the marching claws and hooves of the woodsfolk were about to step into the path of the oncoming city people.

They met on the corner.
Two marching bands of
warriors. Surprise and shock fell
upon the faces of both sides. All of
them stood in silence, for what must
have been only seconds but felt like
forever. And then suddenly the woodsfolk
raced forward and the two groups held their
weapons high and screamed out loud, clashing in
almighty collision. It was not pleasant to hear the crack
of bones or the tear of flesh. Nor to see the spear and
sword cut down the enemy or watch the blood of your
neighbour spill across the snow-white walls of the street
corners. But with war those things come and now
was the hour of many a death.

Horses reared up in the crowd as guardsmen
trampled woodsfolk. Claws raked and wings
flapped. Horned creatures butted their way
through the crowds, cutting down the
city people. Wolves and witches
made their attacks from high and

low and soon the people of the Hollow felt themselves backing away from the foresters, such was their force. Small triumphs and disasters sprung up in pockets of war as the huge fight dispersed into miniature battles.

The fight had edged its way towards the Deadman's Hand and now the street outside its front door was a mass brawl. Inside, its army was separating. As Pip and Frankie headed to the basement, someone else stood at the doorway, ready to join them.

'Billy, no. You're supposed to be resting,' said Pip from under his armour. 'Go back inside. I'm not losing you as well. Not when I've only just found you.'

'I'll not hear of my brother fighting without being by his side,' Billy insisted. 'I'll be fine.' And having watched the others gather anything they could use in the battle, he took hold of a long pointed wooden staff to arm himself.

'OK,' said Pip, admitting defeat, 'but stay by me and don't lose sight of where I am.'

And they disappeared down the hole to the drains.

Back upstairs the troops were banding together to create strength in numbers. About thirty children, packed tightly together, were about to unleash their force.

'Here we go,' said Toad. 'Here comes our favourite customer.' He was now watching carefully through the keyhole of the front door.

Jarvis emerged from the crowds. He was flanked on both sides by bark demons, snapping and snarling as they came. He approached the doorway at the inn and attempted to lift the sneck. The door was locked and so he used the iron handle to rap on the door loudly.

'Little pigs, little pigs, let me come in,' he sneered, laughing out loud, knowing that when they broke down the door and entered he would soon have them in his grasp.

'Ready?' cried Toad.

'Ready!' came a roar.

Unexpectedly the huge door came crashing outwards, knocking Jarvis to the ground and taking his henchmen with him.

Inside the frame stood Toad's army, poised for battle.

All heads turned to see the small band. To most of the woodsfolk, children were a rarity, and for some, they had never been seen before, these small, round-faced versions of the adults they held in such contempt. And for the city folk themselves, in the middle of this mayhem, it was a treat indeed to see children before them. One woman saw her own kin. She cried out in surprise at the sight of Anika and she called to her but her voice was drowned out by the noise. They were only a small group for sure, but it was more children than anyone had seen in a long time.

The woodsfolk seemed to outnumber the city people. Their movement was fast and almost hard to see at times. It made it difficult to engage in battle with them. But the children soon found themselves in the thick of it and without any real choice. They held on to sticks and poles with points that were sharpened into spear tips. They used barrel tops as shields and picked up anything else they could find that might serve as a weapon.

The battle edged itself into the square, the people feeling themselves being pushed back into a defensive position. Witches circled overhead and took swipes as they flew in and out.

Anika had positioned herself near a water pump. Seb noticed and speared his long weapon through the ice to allow the water to break on to the surface. She scooped up half-bucketloads and hurled them at the darting demons. Every now and then she caught one with the water and the puff of blistering smoke came clouding the air.

Jarvis crawled out from under the door and shook himself off, dusting himself down and reattaching his hooked hand.

The city folk were easily outnumbered now and they were being pushed further and further back. Jarvis had seen the power the woodsfolk held over the city and he felt his hour of triumph fast approaching. The city was almost in his hands.

'Is that all you've got?' he laughed out loud.

But Toad and the children's army were determined to spoil his fun.

18

WHERE THE STORY TAKES A TURN

Almost the whole of the city was retreating into the Hollow, the forest smothering them with their attack.

'Come on!' screamed Toad. 'It's now or never. Don't give in!' He looked around him, at his bloodied and bruised companions. He could see that Seb was hurt but that he stood strong.

Below the streets Frankie was leading Pip and Billy through the darkness and calling out. They twisted and turned, this way and that, until Pip felt that he was lost again. Frankie seemed to know the catacombs even better than Toad, it seemed. And then eventually, to Pip and Billy's amazement, a horde of children's faces appeared, and they stepped out into the orange glow of Frankie's flame.

'Well, I did tell you there were more,' she said.

Pip had not expected so many. It was good news. And all of them were armed with sticks and staffs or makeshift swords and heavy batons.

'Ready?' shouted Frankie and her voice echoed through the miles of brickwork.

'Ready!' came a roaring reply that echoed back.

Up above, Toad looked to the ground beneath him and made his way to the nearest drain cover, positioning himself over its wooden lid. Anika found another and did the same and then the rest of the children followed.

'Ready?' roared Toad.

'Ready!' came the answer from all around him.

Toad banged his spear on the wooden drain cover at his feet. *Thud thud thud.*

The sound came back at him like an echo. *Thud thud thud.*

He did it a second time. *Thud thud thud.*

Again it came back. *Thud thud thud.*

The other children followed suit and then, using their makeshift weapons, they dug the sharpened ends under the rims and the drain covers came loose.

From beneath Toad's feet, something began to stir. At first, the wooden lid appeared to lift of its own accord, the movement causing a distraction so that the battle ceased temporarily. What was it that came from beneath the ground of Hangman's Hollow? And now every drain cover followed on, popping up from its place and leaving small holes peppered around the square, each with something stirring beneath simultaneously. The beasts recoiled nervously.

To the surprise of the onlookers Pip climbed out. A wry smile broke across Toad's face. Pip could see that Toad was injured, but he knew that triumph was ahead.

Each lid was thrown aside and from the bowels of Hangman's Hollow children began to climb out in great numbers, all of them armed and all of them ready for victory. One after the other, out they came. Every lost child that had ever been tucked away into a corner of the city returned to take over the streets.

The creatures had backed the city into a corner but now they were surrounded by children in their hundreds. They could not hope to conquer now. The sheer numbers of children were enough to overpower the might of the forest and they attacked from all sides, crushing the power of the woods and herding the beasts

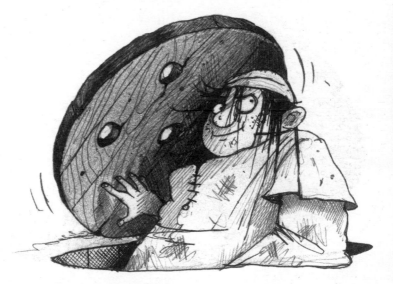

towards the city keep. They were joined by more guardsmen on horseback, driving them into a tightly guarded pack.

One man was tagged on at the back but he tried desperately to sneak away from the group and make his escape. He drifted away beneath the legs of a horse that pushed on from the back and he almost made it. But he was stopped in his tracks.

'Not so fast, Jarvis.'

It was Sam. He had spotted his arch enemy trying to break away with his unmistakeable hooked hand and scarred face. He curled his hand around the scruff of his neck and steered him back into his spot, but not before digging his fist tightly into his ribs and knocking the wind out of his sails, leaving him gasping for breath.

When Jarvis was returned to the crowd he realized he was without his hook, having lost it in the struggle.

'You haven't see the last of me!' he cried out, but Sam could only smile at the sight before him. The weak pathetic figure of Jarvis was even less threatening without his hook. He had been reduced to nothing.

Hector Stubbs approached. 'I'll take over here.' He

grabbed Jarvis unceremoniously by the throat. 'You have some explaining to do, Jarvis. Perhaps you can think things over in your cell and we'll talk in the morning. Take him away,' he shouted as he handed him to the guardsmen.

Toad ran to Sam, throwing his arms around his huge frame, and then Pip and Billy joined them, cheering at their triumph. Frankie ran around, desperately searching, and then a smile broke across her face as the Duprie family surrounded her. The cries died as the forest folk were herded inside the prison walls and cheers replaced the sound as reunions with children and parents were made across the open streets of the city.

Anika and Seb ran breathlessly towards a crowd of aunts and uncles before spotting their weeping parents in the crowd.

For hours on end people wandered around, searching and finding the lost and loved. And it continued into the early hours, each family having its own tale to tell.

As daylight broke the Hollow would change. It would be quick and it would be for the better.

WHERE WE MAY
USE THE EXPRESSION
THE END

The shutters were pulled away from the windows at the Deadman's Hand. It was some time since daylight had been allowed to filter through the small crooked panes. Sam lit the fire and smoke billowed up the chimney, burning off the cobwebs and bringing warmth back into the old place.

The inn was busier now than it had ever been. In

fact, if you took a look outside you'd see that it wasn't the only place to have grown busier. Rub a warm hand across the frosted glass and breathe on to the panes and what you'd see probably isn't what you'd have expected from the Hollow. Children playing in the streets. Market traders wheeling their carts and barrows among the snowy lanes and wood smoke bubbling from the roof pots, throughout the day.

Meanwhile, there was always some tale being told around the fire. Of the days when the forest held its grip over the city and the children who lived in hiding beneath the cobbled walkways in a world of their own helped to save it and restore it back to what it had first been.

Even now someone told their tales around the fire. There was Pip and his brother Billy. There was Toad and Seb and Anika, and in the tall armchair with the decorated scrolls of wood, sat Frankie.

'Tell me again,' said Anika, 'how you escaped from the Duprie family bakery when the creatures came at night.'

'We heard the rattling of the doors,' said Frankie,

'and we thought that the boys were returning, because Pip and Toad had left in search of Billy. But what came through the gap in the wooden entrance as it opened was something dreadful. Bark demons, they were. And they looked and smelled just as grim as they sound.

'I knew the ovens were vented into the catacombs, instead of up the chimney, and we squeezed, all of us, through the flue to emerge into the drains. Believe me, I don't know how we did it. The ovens were still quite

hot and those flues are tiny, but I can tell you, that every morning when I wake and go downstairs to start the ovens, I bless those little chimneys, and not a day goes by without remembering how they saved our lives. We lived some time down in the drains. Without food, and surviving only on the water that melted from the ice.'

Some tales are just too good to be heard only once. A crowd had gathered now and listened in. Adults had gathered around. They too liked to hear the tales, of how their children had saved the city of Hangman's Hollow. They could be proud again now, of their sons and daughters, their nieces and nephews and their grandchildren.

'Here's to all our children,' said Sam, stepping in. 'To the good they bring and in the hope that when we are gone, they will live in times of peace.'

Someone came through the door. Mrs McCreedy. By her side was her proud son Edgar and wrapped in swaddling was her newborn child. 'We thought you might like to say hello to the Hollow's newest addition,' announced Mr McCreedy, stepping in behind her and removing his cap at the door.

'She's beautiful,' said Frankie, and she was suddenly surrounded by adoring children, all keen to get a good look.

'I have something for her,' said Pip.

'What is it, young man?'

Pip dug his hands into his tunic pocket. He pulled out two wooden pegs. They were old and scuffed now, but at one time they had been painted carefully with faces and costumes. He placed them into her tiny hands, her little fingers gripping them hard.

'What are these?'

'Something to help her remember us all,' said Pip. 'It's important to remember.' And he turned to look at his brother.

'Come on, Billy, we have work to do,' he said, and they set off into the city.

THE BIT AT THE VERY END THAT COMES AFTER THE BIT CALLED THE END

The forest was now long gone. Burned to the ground until every last inch of Spindlewood had disappeared into the very bowels of the earth, shrinking back into the hell from which it came.

There was no danger now to the Hollow. Not a single thing, or at least, not unless you count the hard north wind that struck a blow through the maze of alleyways and wound its way around the chimney stacks. Or the deep winter when it came, bringing its share of snow and ice and settling its thick frozen layer upon the river.

But it was spring now and thoughts of winter were far away. Birds sang and the skies brightened, no longer blackened by the cloaks of hags. The season of new growth had begun. Lambs came back to the fields and chickens rattled around the streets between the children playing.

And around the edges of the Hollow, where the blackened ash of the old forest lay, something poked through the dry earth. Green shoots of new life, climbing out from the earthy colours and reaching up to drink in the sunlight.

Chris Mould went to art school at the age of sixteen. During this time, he did various jobs, from delivering papers to washing-up and cooking in a kitchen. He has won the Nottingham Children's Book Award and been commended for the Sheffield. He loves his work and likes to write and draw the kind of books that he would have liked to have on his shelf as a boy. He is married with two children and lives in Yorkshire.

SOMETHING WICKEDLY WEIRD.COM

Praise for the SOMETHING WICKEDLY WEIRD series:

'Engagingly illustrated ...
cheerful, fast-moving romp.'

Carousel

'From the moment they claw their
way out of a graveyard you know
you are onto a winner.'

Publishing News

'A riveting read for newly
independent readers.'

Bookfest

'A splendid mix of Gothic horror
and cartoon-style fun.'

Bookbag

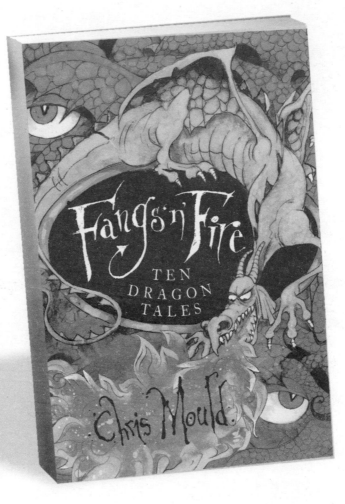

978 0 340 94476 9 £5.99 pb

Beware the dragon ...

This book of fiery dragon tales is adapted,
written and superbly illustrated
by award-winner

Chris Mould

A wonderful collection packed full of fangs
and fire, dragon myths and legends:
from *George and the Dragon* to the
Chinese myth *The Eyeless Dragons*

Open this book at your own peril ...